NUCLEAR LOVE

NUCLEAR LOVE

Eugene Wildman

THE SWALLOW PRESS INC.
1139 S. WABASH AVENUE CHICAGO, ILLINOIS 60605

Copyright © 1972 by Eugene Wildman
All rights reserved
Printed in the United States of America

First Edition

This book is printed on 100% recycled paper.

ISBN (CLOTHBOUND EDITION) 0-8040-0568-0
ISBN (PAPERBOUND EDITION) 0-8040-0569-9
LIBRARY OF CONGRESS CATALOG CARD NUMBER 70-189193

Portions of this book have previously appeared
in the *Chicago Review*.

Adapted from *The Rise and Fall of Maya
Civilization*, by J. Eric S. Thompson. Copyright
1954 by the University of Oklahoma Press.

This book is dedicated to
Shirley Sarris, without whose sensitivity and help nothing
would have been written down.
Alain Arias-Misson, prophet, chronicler of our Vietnam
Superfiction, author of *Vietnam-Superfiction*.

The boy without an ego who lived in Chopin's house. Chopin kept getting better and better, and the boy without an ego had to practise the harmonica in the park at night. Winter came. Ice formed around the reeds. It kept on getting colder, until the boy without an ego froze to death.

Because Chopin decided to move in above him.

"When I'm home I sleep until 9:30 or 10, and then Mom brings me breakfast in bed," he says.

"I sit in my chair for a couple of hours, or get up on my litter and watch television. I read. I listen to records — Tom Jones, rock, country-western.

"Days go by. Sometimes it surprises me how fast four years can go by like this. Then I

think of 10 more years going by. I'll still be a young man, 33. . . ."

The Newspaper That Sells The Truth

(Rue's voice reading)
. . . they came again at dawn. They cut us up badly. Look! the newspapers are able to speak for themselves.

(Star reading)
Author tells all. My father you know was a genius, his mind lay like wide open and I could look down into it just like into the sea. But he had this thing you know. I would come home in the evening, the living room would be dark. I would start to turn on a lamp but he would be there. He would be sitting there in the living room and I would hear him. He would be across the living room in a bound saying I'll do it and he would snap the switch on. Then I would hear the switch go on. It would happen this thing, this sort of thing whenever I would chance to come home in the dark. It is very important you know, it is very important that people should turn on their own lamps.

(Rue's voice again)
. . . the teachers are gone now, they are gone because they

taught students to give the wrong answers. Pigs want the right answers, whoever wants the right answer is a pig. What do they mean by the right answer anyway? What do they mean by teaching anyway? So they let them go, dismiss them. Teachers are always losing their jobs for telling students the wrong answers. That's why Jimi burned his guitar. That's why the Greeks killed Socrates. Jimi lives. Socrates lives. They're dead.

(*Star*)

Has but one maxim to give. You are only free when you struggle to be free.

(*Rue*)

. . . when you can turn around and walk away from it, burn it.

When I remember you it is in the present, now. You are holding our child. You are an Indian bride. We say nothing, we are staring at each other across two different times. I am looking at my hands. My hands have changed so. If we could only divest ourselves some way, take ourselves back. We do not belong here. I call your name in the present. Teloca. Teloca. Teloca.

These words do not convey the present, do not convey the
time inside us. We do not belong among these strangers, Teloca,
always speaking their words, always thinking in their mind.
I was glad when the bishops ordered our books burned. There
is nothing these strangers have not stolen. These Europeans.
There are so many words rushing through my veins. Look!
my eyes have turned blue. How is it that my eyes have become
blue? Look at my body, I was born to walk across deserts,
to survive the famine and the drought. How is it that I have
come to live here and do not know my own mind? Our thoughts
have melted with our gold Teloca, those strangers have taken
everything and melted it. Those Europeans. And their country
that they call by a different name. They have made us forget
our minds. They have cheated us of our time Teloca.

(Teloca)
They fattened us with *reasons*.

(Odessa)
They burned themselves secretly in our *flesh*.

(Teloca)
They *changed* us.

(Odessa)
Our *eyes* have become different.

(Teloca)
Everything was done for *reasons*.

(Odessa's voice reading)

. . . beginners in going into it. This is what it is, it begins to expand, you begin to feel differently, this is really exactly where we are . . . now . . .

(The spectators are in darkness. We stand in light surrounded
by this darkness. To the spectators we seem the elect. They
regard us as chosen people, more real than they are somehow.
We ourselves feel differently of course. We view ourselves
merely as shadows. Where do these shadows come from, these
reduced realities? Our dominating concern is with our unreality.
We give ourselves names, we take on roles, but still we feel
ourselves to be shadows. We project this essence into the
darkness. We can hardly see any longer in these surroundings
but we can easily distinguish our voices from yours. Sound
is almost the only quality in our lives. It seems often as if
our existence depends entirely on our speech. We understand
that you perceive us as voices, though we do not know if our
roles are inferior to yours. We want only to exist on the same
level as the spectators. We are forced to choose our words with
so much care. Everything that keeps us from being spectators
is experienced by us as pain.)

We are in a hospital where they only play the records of
dead people and have posters of the dead hanging from the
walls. We are being taught something. I hate the way they
wait outside the doors listening for the pop of the revolver. So
they can come in after and get on with the job of cleaning up.
Teloca we have been wandering for what seems like centuries.
I know that we have come to another country. I can scarcely
imagine that we could be separated by cities. Do you remember
how all the dogs began running at once? And the railroad
tracks were filled by them? There was a panic in their brains.
There was a concentration on their faces. Teloca I want to
dance with you. I want us to dance seriously, with our motion
held inside. The wolf has entered the village Teloca, there is
blood all over its teeth. Do you remember when we walked
among swans along the water, how spectral they became, how
they began to whisper like ancestors telling us things, telling
us what there was to fear, telling us what we had to part from?
We have to dance until the exterior becomes still, seems dead,
seems a mask. Until finally the exterior is all inside, swallowed
up. It is the only way we will survive.

(Dog)

In knowledge. After waiting 13 months for something it began again at last. I began at last. I had amazing energy, I understood the past, I understood that something had been growing in me. Then I looked down and saw the tumor.

(Teloca)

We have run out of time.

(Odessa)

This is what death is: energy. Somewhere someone has terminated us. We are still living and there is no more time.

(Teloca)

We are into the dance. How blue your eyes are.

CLUMP 2

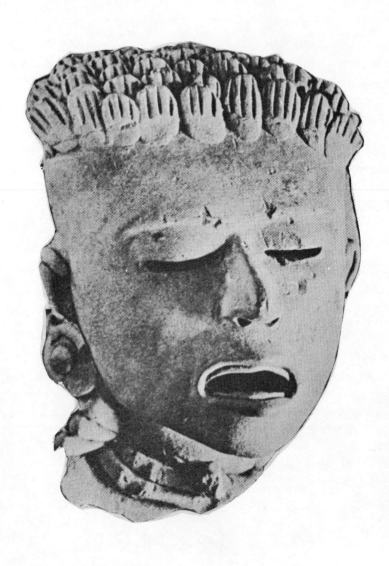

"First the hands betray you. Then the rest of the body opens, blossoming flowers everywhere, the body has no more places to hide. At night, in secret, meticulously, you strike back with razor, the hunting knife is put by the bed table. And when at last the worm betrays you, with what knife will you cut into the outrage? The spirit is dead. The body is beginning. Thickness will teach you, when the worm is dead. When the worm is dead, thickness will become god."

"In the Reality Beggars Theater they take your razor away. Consequently they are preoccupied with locks and with hiding. It is part of the treatment. They speculate about my life in Paris. They wonder how much French I know, but everyone has been paid to listen to *them*. It is a form of theater to live here, I have begged in here before. The cure is fishing, for which they need worms. The doctors have all had the same education. We are here because we have the blues."

"We were dropped in here."

"No one ever gave me a choice."

"I remember a blond girl with pale, vacant eyes. The crowd had formed a circle around me. A man with enormous hands came out of the crowd and began walking toward me. Somehow I was aware of her eyes on him. I could see the vacant look in them, and the lips, which were slightly open. Then he put his hand on my head . . . and squeezed it. 'It's alright,' they said to me afterward. 'I can feel it inside,' I told them. . . 'Something is coming out. I can feel my intelligence oozing out.' "

"In Majhi's hands I found my real truth and my real destiny. Majhi, who would never tolerate a prick inside her,

15

whose tolerance for my lassitude has turned into a demand
that I rent a room in her apartment, to be visited by her at
her will, after and during customers. Where warmth of her
hands will rouse the cold worm from his sleeping place. Where
ceaselessly, with a fascination that dominates her, in darkness
or in black light that turns my vision blue, light that slows
detail, her hands grapple with time and my night. Those
possessing fingers touch my time, lift me, stretch me, her
yawning hand consumes my sleeping, her hand is the hand
that eats inside my darkness."

"Listen. Inside my mind is a mesopotamian awareness
that is fully conscious. These blue eyes I look out at you with
belonged to the black sailor who raped my great-grandmother
in Warsaw's Ghetto. It's the only visible feature I inherited from
that great-grandfather who was black. What do you imagine
you have to say to these eyes?"

"Teloca and I fell from Eden together. The feeling of
time was so strongly upon me, perhaps because we knew there
was so little left to us. There was nothing we could say. We
walked there by the lake, near that same Peacock Garden I had
gone to with my father when I was a boy. We walked aimlessly,
occasionally our eyes touching, our fingers. Then, tacitly
agreeing, eyes or fingers would separate, withdraw. We
returned to ourselves, to our absence of thoughts, and mingled
with the swans along the water's edge. They were inviolate
in their aloofness, in their claim to purposelessness, in their

16

rights of possession of the water and its banks. We were inferior to such strength and legitimacy. 'Touch it!' a woman taunted her husband, smiling, knowingly, pointing to one of the large males. The powerful neck flashed forward, the heavy wings flapped twice. The birds were gigantic, white. We suddenly became aware of how few of us there were. The beak snapped. The swan hissed like an angry cat, the wings flapped again. Another hissed and snapped its beak at the air. Three swans began to walk upon the lake, candles borne upon the water. The remainder, there must have been more than twenty we realized all at once, sullenly drove us from the bank. We left the park, I can still see the reddish flaring of the sun."

"Are these stories true?"

"I was told about a man who helped the Germans make the selections so that his daughter wouldn't have to go to a doll house. She was the first one the Germans sent through. How do we measure the value of an idea? How many reasons are given for it? 'What are your *reasons*?' the people demanded. He was surrounded, he was standing on the exact center. For a long time he wouldn't answer. A man's world had ended and he was still dissembling. A vision was coiled inside that was only waiting to be unleashed. 'I was afraid she would like it,' he said, and then went on living."

"Do you think any of that happened?"

"What have we got to go by? In the stories it happens over and over again."

CLUMP 3

```
                    A
    M                          LOVE
            HATE                        L
        HATE          P            O
P       O                   HATE
        M         TIME  M
        E    CREATE      M    DESTINY
    O   TIME               M              ME
        ME      M  DESTINY        DEST RO   I
STOP  X  I  DES  TROY        KILLOVE        O
       O   TRO  INY   S    ME    S    STOP
   NOR     ME   E   LOVE      S
       GO   M E        TIME  CREATE      M
       R  Z  R O START  ME    BREATH TIME
HATE        O O  OR          STOP ME
ME      M      TIME   ME  NO   S  STOP LOVE
ME       SNAKE      ME      LOVE     ME
        L  CREATE  WINDOW
BE M IN KILL    SEE P      STOP    O    V
  EF EVE VE  ME   STAR    N      A
   SEA      TIME      ME         V
HATE    DEST  I  NY   TIME
              DESTINY         LOVE
    TIME  DESTROY            NO
         TIME              NOV A
KILL        NOW   CREATE      E
   O                              I
TIME   M  V  E    ME            T
M      M   E             N  E       M   E
   E      E          H  A  T  O
```

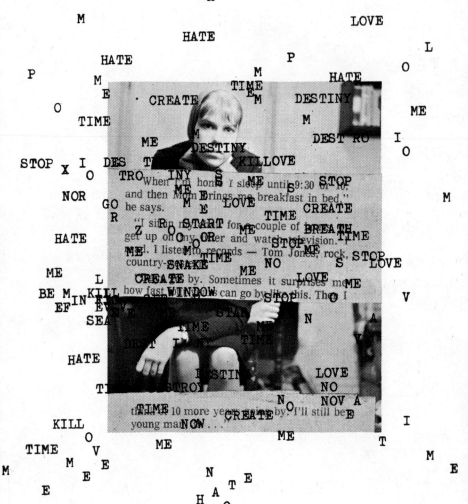

BLUE WOMB

The dining room of a Grand Hotel. Solid bourgeois plush.
Entertainment. While being entertained, the guests are eating
desserts, drinking coffee, relaxing. Juju has curly red
hair, is of medium height and stocky build, muscular and
tending slightly toward flab. He is nude except for a jockstrap
and a well-stuffed knapsack on his back. He struts rather than
walks, and his manner is altogether arrogant. The dining
room goes from left to right across the stage. Juju is at
the front, stage left. All the way to the rear, stage right, on a
slightly raised dais, is Odessa. His hair is dark, he wears a
perfectly trimmed goatee, a black and white-checked jacket,
and is sipping from a glass of red wine. He constantly takes
his napkin, which is white linen, and pats his lips with it.
Before patting his lips, however, he is fairly conspicuous about
rolling it into a ball first. A second guest worth noting is a
thin, aristocratic and at the same time very dissipated-looking
man. He is very nervous, constantly pushing his hair back and
moistening his lips with his tongue. Last, a woman, extremely
overdressed, middle to late thirties, wearing a red dress with
which she has combined a chain necklace with a Byzantine
cross strikingly outlined with pearls.

Juju: I may say, without delivering a polemic upon the
subject, that in the last decade our attitude toward the body has
undergone a fundamental change. There are things we take for
granted now which once, astonishing though it may seem, all
our instincts would have tempted us to deny. For example, these
childish bodies of ours, the sight of which we once considered
so provocative that one is forced to conclude they must have
been regarded as a challenge to something deep within us. Or
to some deeply venerated belief we held, perhaps without even

(Teloca)

We have run out of time.

The dining room of a Grand Hotel. Solid bourgeois plush.
Entertainment. While being entertained, the guests are eating
desserts, drinking coffee, relaxing. Juju has curly red
hair, is of medium height and stocky build, muscular and

(Odessa)

This is what death is: energy. Somewhere someone has
terminated us. We are still living and there is no more time.

tending slightly... man
walks, and his manner is altogether arrogant. The dining
room goes from left to right across the stage. Juju is at
the front, stage left, all the way to the rear, stage right, on a
slightly raised dais, is Odessa. His hair is dark, he wears a

(Teloca)

We are into the dance. How blue your eyes are.

perfectly... jacket,
and is sipping from a glass of red wine. He constantly takes
his napkin, which is white linen, and pats his lips with it.
Before patting his lips, however, he is fairly conspicuous about
rolling it into a ball first. A second guest worth noting is a
... at the same time very dissipated-looking
man. He ... constantly pushing his hair back and
moistening ... with ... Last, a woman extremely
overdressed ... middle ... wearing a red dress with
which she has combined a chain necklace with a Byzantine
cross strung ... with pearls.

Juju: I may say, without delivering a polemic upon the
subject, that in the last decade our attitude toward the body has
undergone a fundamental change. There are things we take for
granted now which once, astonishing though it may seem, all
our instincts would have tempted us to deny. For example, these
childish bodies of ours, the sight of which we once considered
so provocative that one is forced to conclude they must have
been regarded as a challenge to something deep within us. Or
to some deeply venerated belief we held, perhaps without even

(Teloca)

We have run out of time.

The dining room of a Grand Hotel. Solid bourgeois plush. Entertainment. While being entertained, the guests are eating desserts, drinking coffee, relaxing. Juju has curly red hair, is of medium height and stocky build.

(Odessa)

moment of truth due

walks, and his manner is altogether arrogant. The dining room goes from left to right across the stage. Juju is at the front, stage left, all the way to the rear, stage right, on a slightly raised dais, sits Odessa. His hair is dark, he wears a perfectly trimmed goatee, a black and white checked jacket,

(Teloca)

We are into the dance. How blue your eyes are.

and is sipping from a glass of red wine. He constantly takes his napkin, which is white linen, and pats his lips with it. Before patting his lips, however, he is fairly conspicuous about rolling it into a ball first. A second guest worth noting is a thin, aristocratic but at the same time very dissipated-looking man. He is nervous, constantly pushing his hair back and moistening his lips with his tongue. Last, a woman extremely overdressed, middle-to-late thirties, wearing a red dress with which she has combined a chain necklace with a byzantine cross strikingly laced with pearls.

Plan unveiled

Juju: I may venture, without being dogmatic upon the subject, that in the last decade our attitude toward the body has undergone a fundamental change. There are things we take for granted now which once, astonishing though it may seem, all our instincts would have tempted us to deny. For example, these childish bodies of ours, the sight of which we once considered so provocative that one is forced to conclude they must have been regarded as a challenge to something deep within us. Or to some deeply venerated belief we held, perhaps without even

CLUMP 4

(You perpetuate this unreality. We have no way of seeing past these lights you blind us with in order that *you* may be able to see. *Our helplessness is your light.* Do you imagine these impersonations you ask for can be anything but a light that causes confusion? You want us to represent you as merchants who wash the feet of the doomed. That degradation be elevated: you ask only that of the theater. You come to the theater to be forgiven. An anxiety is inside this theater. It covers us all. Do you have any idea what these impersonations cost us? An Aztec victim was permitted to make a speech. While we, who also are doomed, must speak for you and be spoken for by others. You are unlike us! We cannot go on speaking for each other. It is wrong for victims to *seem* to be having their feet washed. There cannot be holy merchants. Commerce is not astronomy. A living heart has been torn out and the flesh has been refused. We have almost no sense of you. We are unable to see into those shadows.)

Polis 1. Arraignment of the Policeman Khaber Chaud for Failure to Sound His Staff. There was no reason for it. It accomplished nothing. It absented sound from one quadrant. Think of the terror of terrorized people. Think of activities stopping in the quadrant. **People were forced.** People were hearing
what they were accustomed to not hearing.
Policemen are required to sound their staffs. One staff did not sound
Four is the crucial number. One of four did not sound.

The day on which an event occurs must be taken into account.
Three was made dominant over
four. People believed that heaven had failed them.
Three is an unaccustomed sound.

Policeman Khaber Chaud did those things. He did them on the day of a mad god. To a lack of sound he added three. It is too
unlucky a day for three.
Three was made dominant over four.
People believed that heaven had fallen.

Polis 2. Inquest Following the Disturbance at the Card House. The Violence That Was Done to Blanche Neige, Resident of the Card House, by the Teacher Wild. Alleged. He had referred to the Card House unflatteringly. Deposition. It is a Card House. It is a Card House like others. Testimony of the Teacher Wild. The inner necessity of her was too strong. Objections. Denied. Others must be acted upon by outer force. Her necessity is too strong, she grows silently, she dances against my being, her hard dancing

offends my teachness.

Blanche Neige was not one of us. All well and good. I could tell right away she would have begun dancing. I was able to know this. She wrote a story called The Soft Prince. I knew The Soft Prince would have become a dance. This was not our way. I am Teacher. I know best. I was required to be stern for those reasons. There should not be dancing in the Card House. Or else the Card

House will fall. And once again we will have nowhere to be.

Can Blanche Neige return? Things have to remain. In order that we can find words, speech eventually. You have no language? No language. Foreign speech. An outside. A discarded wrapping of old language. **We have only old words.** There is now no way

of speaking each to other.

28

Conclusion of
The Hot Times

(Blanche)

Women have none of these abstractions that trouble you so. Women live so much more vividly. We give ourselves. That is why we are able to be superior in love.

(Star)

I sometimes feel the shaking of this country, the land, itself . . . we cannot possibly endure our language . . . words are explosions in such a terribly . . . terribly , . . tenuous reality . . . can we possibly be so stupid, not to realize there are consequences . . . and then we say it . . . we . . .

(Blanche)

You know that your pleasure never equals ours. You always know it. I used to dream of making love for 2,864 nights consecutively. Many women make love for 2,000 nights in a row. I myself make love every single night. I find that I no longer count . . . persons . . .

(Star)
. . . the newspapers are always correcting themselves . . .
correcting reality . . . names, appropriateness of the *errors* . . .
I don't see how we can possibly endure any more . . .

(Blanche)
   You immolate yourselves inside our sex . . . poor sacrificial dolls
. . . because you think falling is always into time . . . *down* into
time . . . it starts me burning to think of it . . . being touched . . .
how hard existent things are . . .

(Star)
   How soft reality is . . . how hard words can become next
to it, inside it all right . . . how can we know our choices . . . a
word will take on a meaning . . . many years later sometimes . . .
someone may become enraged . . .

(Blanche)

As we walked by holding hands all the swans that had gathered along the bank suddenly began shrieking at once: "Europe! Europe!" I swear this happened . . . I could never bear him within me again . . . afterward . . . all you offer are fantasies . . .

CLUMP 5

They beat me because I was playing their music. This is my
music too, I said. They clustered around me. *Look!* I said.
My eyes are blue! Did this happen in Warsaw? Did this
happen in Marrakesh? Anyplace at all. It is this business of
contexts that gets it confusing. They began to hit me, the way
the motherfuckers do me everywhere. I fell to the ground with
my arms stretched out, like the figures of my people that the
others carry everywhere, dangling from chains around their
necks, our arms nailed to the wood. They carry us on chains
that hang around their necks!

When they were finished I got up and walked home. Oh
Jesus: die for me. Oh Jesus: die for me. Put
yourself on your cross, *eat* it. I played Miles. I followed
in a long high line, all alone, I'm always alone, just Miles and
me stretching out, miles and miles and miles of high, all I have
is that long thin line, miles and miles and miles of Miles, he
blowing it and me blowing it back with the only thing I have,
that high desert wail, a trumpet and a jews harp.
Stupid, isn't it? *Fuck* you. Juju will get you. This is my
confession: *I* am the Jesus of your life.

It is the business of contexts that gets everything confused.
I spend so much of my time inside of metaphors. Peter and
Emily and I, we are standing by the kitchen window. The
scenario has been avoided so far. We all know it. That's what
being hung-up means: crucified. And then Emily pulls up the
window. "I took your music away? Fine. You don't have
any music anymore." She waves her arm. Grandiose bitch.
Peter, who has seen the cross of my eye, pulls it down. Emily,
who has seen that music go before, raises it back up.

I have no more reality here. There are no clocks in this apartment. In my house there are three clocks, each set at a different time. I never remember their relation to each other. I continue to wear my watch even though it has been broken for weeks. Each time the window goes up or down I have to change the field of reference. I no longer have any orientation. I have no way of telling how I am required to react. I am an old Indian. I am beginning to moult. I have always wanted to be a Mayan. I will end up being the Serpent from the East.

I am going to change a lot of things. I am going to change nothing. In the end of course I do not jump out of the context. Peter slams the window shut. Which doesn't mean that I still don't have to face a fall and a cross.

(Eyes)

A young Sioux is laughing derisively, telling how he and some friends made a papier mache cross, and hung a papier mache Indian on it. But something got crossed between his head and mine. That's right, you pig motherfucker, I thought. You dig it, go up it yourself. It ain't gonna be us *for* you. And all the time television flashing, something about living on time, living it out inside the rain. Culminating with the fears, culminating with the opening of a *Flash Cab* door, culminating with the opening of my right eye.

In the other room Helen sleeps or waits. This is the fourth year that I have not found a way to do it. Fall. Depression makes me willful perhaps. I am an old Indian. I am a bagful

34

of nits and sores. I am on. I am off. I have white thoughts,
I have black thoughts. I am so many people. I am a living
theater.

I have been to Europe. Twice. I carried bags. My hands
grew sore. They grew willful. They clenched. They were fists
to shake at the sky. They were balloons that floated in the
sky. Left is my ego, right is my id. They are balloons that
never rise above me.

Which side of me is it sleeping on? Does it, he, look like me?
No. Like my death. I have written these words and I will be
reading them elsewhere within six months. It is like living on
the doorsill of the underworld. It keeps happening, like an
event in a dream, that keeps you from waking. I would like
to write a book about this, but if I started to do it, it would
appear within a month. There is some kind of dynamo that
I am plugged into, that has made this keep on happening.
The dynamo, like one's death, is a fact.

I tell you something strange about Europe. Turn left twice
to get out of Germany. There's the hidden idea. Take your
cue from the rooming house locks. Right closes in. Left opens
out.

After midnight the first-class riders on the Metro become
uneasy. The police are stiff, guilty-looking. Afraid of trouble.
The second-class people enter the first-class cars. They have
room for once, they relax. The women are not ashamed of
their men. Above the Metro the avenues radiate like immense
ideas in Mandel's Wheel. Paris, again, dreams the Wheel,

35

becomes the Wheel, becomes Logic, becomes the Vicious Circle. Beneath these abstractions on the surface, the Metro produces an interior logic. Those who are afraid to close their eyes suffocate. With eyes open the first-class people shudder and dream of the Metro closing down in the dark.

(Breakage)

Most of my life has been spent around underworlds. When you live near the entrace to the underworld, everything in life becomes breakable. There is no difference between glass and emotion. Shelves are a necessity.

Once in New York I lived literally above the underground. The glass jars in my kitchen were in constant movement. Every four days they came to the edge of the shelf and had to to be pushed back. I slept on a mattress, the only furniture. The only other furniture was unpacked cartons. I made coffee and put it on the floor by the mattress. Stretched on the mattress, I leaned my head over and lapped at the coffee. Like an animal.

Every morning the landlord was out in front of the building. The building was his pet, the tenants were its food. When I saw him through the window an unease rose up in me, and to make sure, I put on a tie. Whatever the weather, I kept the top button of my coat open so that he saw I was wearing a tie. One day I left that mattress and that landlord. Split. Before leaving I pushed the glass things back from the edges. I went down into the subway. That's how it is near the entrance.

In the case of my hands, there was never much to be hoped for. And dissembling has become impossible now. My hands, from so much walking, have become large and worn, useless extensions of luggage.

Pieces of baggage like myself cannot be hidden between knees. Fists as large as suitcases only become conspicuous when they try to become invisible. Like my slavery to Majhi, there is only the rawness of myself. Nothing exquisite. No abstractions. A pair of fists as large as suitcases exists only in the realm of phenomena. A life that has been used like a suitcase can pretend to only certain ideals. Other ideals have to have other lives.

(Dreams)

In Europe, people fold as simply as paper, and are called therefore asleep. While inside the Gare du Nord, a clock is ticking the moments of Paris, in time to the moving of a serpent shedding somewhere in a Brazilian rainforest.

In spite of this the Chequers appear. Twitchy, hiding wealth all over themselves, riddled with doubt and contradiction in exact proportion, staying at the Hilton for security one night, hating themselves and staying at the train station the next, they trust no one, terrified to go first class (your luggage is checked—by the poor!), then traveling second and even third class. Everyone of course is a thief, watching slyly, cautiously feeling for those concealed lumps, those envelopes of money and traveller's cheques, tumors of paranoia.

I thought I knew what paranoia was before, until I bought a French jacket. Pockets all over. With buttons. Before that I just carried my money. If I was going to get robbed, I was going to get robbed. It was something that

37

happened. Then I bought that jacket. A fine jacket. The French have a definite sense of style. But it isn't possible to have a pocket without wanting to put something in it. The first time you do it, that's it. You put something in a pocket, you have something to hide. You put a button on that pocket and you've put a time limit on your sanity.

(Dreams)

The Chequers watch from their cafes, without comment or comprehension, as the snake, Europe, well-dressed and growing old, sheds its worn skin. Europe is burning and no one notices or yells fire. This archaic homeland is burning its way out of its skin and the new serpent is wriggling free. Like the serpent when the lips of Majhi part, this serpent with its double tongue is rising, sipping coffee.

(A sign informs me in French: 60 Min. Max. What can one say? Right on, Max!) There are two Europes and they are growing apart. There are two Americas and they are growing into each other. Slowly. So as not to burn. So as not to burn our own flesh. We have to face our fires with· the fortitude of Indians.

I keep rushing to the station to produce passports and cash cheques. Preferring to risk what is on the way in the streets to the unnameables of the locker at the station; which seals its lips, and closes its expression, and pretends to sleep after midnight. You are lost once you have pockets with buttons. You are always rushing, afraid of midnight. Your dreams are transformations of closed lockers.

(Dreams)

At noon when the bells are unloosed, you can hear it: the difference. The Walloons, having turned to stone already,

38

fear no more changes. The energy in the twisted coils of
the serpent is as irresistible and as far beyond individual
will as the music of the bells in the impeccably appropriate
stone squares. Quetzalcoatl has bestowed his flowers.

Under the bottoms of our feet, Majhi, our faces are the
earth. Should fools know that death is green? We are seated
atop an iceberg that is racing toward the equator.

I need to marry a whore. But for whose redemption?
It is not as if Jews invented the style, but we took
it over like a neighborhood is overrun. So I will never be
happy unless I marry a whore.

(Rider)

Time is here laughing, slowly slowly heaving itself
up, a burden unto itself, a sound like the sound of a rattle, a
sound like a finger moving across a drum.

I learned that at the Louvre. The Louvre is a gyp: the
complete education. The Greek philosophers are all old
men looking for handouts. (Chrysippe.) A scroll without a
head. (Thales.) And Apollo. Where the eyes meet you, the
mouth is too distant for prophesy. When the lips seem ready
to speak, the eyes are already fixed on something beyond.

The real philosophy is being made on the trains. Some
nights it is impossible to get a hotel, so I ride the trains on
those nights. In every second-class car there are empty seats
marked Reservée. The first-class cars are almost totally
empty. In the narrow aisles outside the cabins are people
without seats. Arabs. The first other Semites I have ever seen.
They sit in the cramped aisles on their suitcases, we stare,
nomads careening through Europe on a destiny train.

Here are two different worlds meeting. I was taught in
high school the meaning of Reservée. I am totally

unintimidated by those signs. When I see them I throw them out the windows and invite the world to enter the cabins. Those Arabs, whose French is far better than mine, have been taught to read them in a far different way. It is my world. But I know also where the real lines have been drawn. Which is why, on my sorties into the first-class cars, I go alone, careful to invite no one. We all have crucifixion backgrounds. Whores and reserved seats.

I exorcise my bad conscience by thinking about the Louvre. All those statues of ancient Greeks. All the eyes are taken out or blanked. The mouths are all open insinuatingly. Chamber after chamber of screw-in socket-pricks, of peg-leg heroes, of a headless woman, one leg up, cunt on a pedestal.

(Clouds)

Near the Champs Elysées a black man is lying face down in the street. He looks . . . dead. So stiff. He could go into the Louvre tomorrow. And there he would be. Dead.

I love you, dead man. Why do you have to be dead for me to love you?

I feel: I have no way of holding that music in my
head. I rush so as not to forget the song. Across the street,
at the Cafe Terminus, he sits there, the keeper of the terminus.
"Rambo, can you write this?" I hum it for him. A short song.
He nods wearily and takes out a pad. For six francs he
writes it down. Two francs more and he plays it for me,
making suggestions about the rhythm. We have been doing
this business for a long time. "God bless you, Rambo." Don't
die, Rambo.

(Dancers)

The moment I put my hand in the pocket of my European
jacket, this dissolves. The risks are too great for me not to
play the harp myself. I will have to keep my own music.
To myself. These were never my Apaches; I will always be
a tourist here.

CLUMP 6

London is a masque, with its music, with its blues. What
happens to civilizations: their theaters take them over entirely.
The theater is the last subject anyone can afford to be frank
about in England.
(My hands did
Not turn out
At all the way I had expected
While I was distracted by
Looking at other things)
London is a series of vanishing points to which you must
always return. You will never cease being found. But the
risk of disorientation is too great. For example, they are
doing the Theater of Hunger right now. The restaurants are in
pairs. They have different names over the entrances. You
pass by one, because of the prices, and go into the next.
The waiter comes in through a curtain. The waiters and
waitresses are all recently arrived Spaniards who act
traumatized by the fact that their customers are speaking to
them in English. Wimpy's is especially involved in this
strange oral duality. I sit in the London Grill House,
watching the waiter pass through the curtain with food from
Wimpy's kitchen, for which he charges me Grill House prices.
There is one play, the tickets vary. If I attempt to speak to
him, he becomes traumatized.
Everyone has a place in a world of his own, beyond which
he knows nothing. Four blocks from London University is
a post office, whose personnel are unable to tell me where
the university is. They pore over my map, pointing out
landmarks to each other. How can you *not* know?"
I ask exasperatedly. "I have no *need*

to know," I am answered haughtily. A block away from the underground I ask a man where the closest entrance is. "There *is* no underground on *this* street," he chastizes, continuing on his way. "Are there any coffee shops nearby?" I ask one man who is coming out of one. "I'm sorry, I don't know," he replies, and walks on. A strange theater of hunger.

The artists in the present are going to the museums and demanding equal time and space with Rembrandt. What is Europe anyway? The mayors would rather close the museums. But they are really not sure if they are locking themselves in or out. Eventually they will give them equal time. Anything to escape life in the present.

Looking at those crumpled figures in the Metro, it seems like the last day on earth. Why are we not speaking news? Why is Rambo not singing here? Why is the truth not proclaimed at every moment? When will we learn to read the newspapers in the here and now?

(Camera)

She climbs atop the exhausted monument. Opens the photo album like a pair of cheeks. And thrusts in his face fine girls, nubile and hot, many and young. The monument is restored. Her breasts harden from her own satisfaction. The true artist can change your life. Continuous performances. Best act in town. Stop.

CLUMP 7

This period is of 52 years and 365 days. It is called Round Time. There are, therefore, 18,980 different combinations of day name, day number and month position in Round Time. The gods of 4, 7, 9, and 13 are kindly disposed. Those of 2, 3, 5, and 10 are malign. Ahau is the day as well as the sun. Both are gods. A man born on the day of the god dog will stray from home often. 4 is the number of a man's life. Time may be re-entered by the god 13 Ahau. I am descended from a god. 9 corn yields treasure. It is getting very late. I am feeling very tired.

46 leap days have been added since July 4, 1776. Had we done as was formerly done and made no correction, we would celebrate July 4 when the sun rises where it normally rises on May 19. With the passing of centuries July 4 would be falling in mid-winter. In the course of 19 centuries the feast of Christmas would be celebrated on every day of the year. Easter, ruled by the spring equinox, would fall around July. Independence Day would come between Christmas and Easter. An orderly nature dreads such conditions. To live is to accumulate error. The task of the living is to calculate and record accumulated error. The gods will destroy the world one day. These records will be the only way of keeping track of the good and the evil that was done.

CLUMP 8

624 (Shield). The associations are not clear. Money at Palenque. Sometimes close to records of 4 or 5 20-year spans. The propeller element is really an infix. The variant with the checkerboard infix is of interest because checkerboards are of interest. Arrivals and departures are uncertain. Checkerboards are uncertain as main signs.

670 (Hand with other sign in corner). The compound with the sky sign has a very wide distribution. No. 90 is of interest because the sky sign is beneath the hand, not resting on it. The hand is resting on the sky. It is perhaps holding something back.

I can't handle the fragmentation anymore. Certain conjunctions are unlucky. I must remember. There are certain unlucky conjunctions . . . each number can have any attribute . . . for reasons that must always be calculated in advance. A patient man is never surprised . . . there is too much to keep in mind . . .

CLUMP 9

When I go from here, I will be leaving the museum-library chain and returning to the hospital chain. This is on my mind, a weight, a literal pull on my mind.

The "chosen man" is the Priest. For me it has to begin and end with that. Open with him. Then my mind can again be me, on the train, watched by Arabs and by Europeans, with the hospital corridors waiting.

Me as Entertainer, literally, walking around their Europe, juju returned.

It has become Roi vs. Kafka. No one is chosen forever or is the drum forever. It will be fought in the sun rooms and in the corridors of the ward— and Roi will be the Doctor, armed with his ways and his syringe.

It has been a long battle fought among Michelangelo's statues, Van Gogh in the museum vs. Acid, in the Prado, in the Louvre, in the sky above Toledo.

Consciousness keeps coming back to Spain, goes there and always settles there again. Spain of greed, Spain of death, Spain of Basques, of Anarchists, of Morrocams, of Indians, of Gypsies, of Africans. Old Worlds, New Worlds. A meeting of calendars. A crossing of year lines.

At the end of this *Inferno Now* a Mayan priest emerges from the Guatemalan jungle and demands the sacred books which were stolen and removed to Dresden, Paris, Madrid.

"Chosen" may mean only going to bring them back. Europe may deserve to endure for no more than only that reason.

Certainly when you get there you wonder why you have come,
what sane or even insane purpose you might have had.
At the end, a Mayan priest *does* emerge.
"Chosen" means "chosen" only as agent—to steal the ms. from
the Dresden library and return it to the People.

This is what "return" means.

Europe has been made sick inside by its crimes. To return
the ms. will remove the curses from its people; and from
me and from my own people, the Affliction.

Now I feel that I am moving south. With my puma shoes,
with my red puma warm-up shoes. I am looming on the ice,
I am coming on the sun. I am headed for a magnetic
intersection at the center of a tropical rain forest, where a
priest named Rue waits with absolute certainty, beneath a
tree that ages before already had been chosen.

CLUMP 10

How we came to leave the trains, how we came to sail on barges. The beginning of riding underground, the beginning of singing inside the earth.

"I feel we must be victims of something. But I don't know what."

"Of our stories."

He sat there on the ward with us. He explained how he got there.

"I withdrew. Some sort of current took me on it."

"We have to take everything back, all feeling, faces are wood, mask, eyes wood, mask, perfectly hidden, mask, *now* die, *now*. Only we know what *this* withdrawing is, this gathering, this absence, celebrated together."

"We have all taken ourselves back. How else did we get to be here?"

We can feel that Roi is in the room somewhere. We can tell his breathing. It is different from ours, harsh against our different minds.

"Even before you came, I was trying to write withdrawal prose. I was getting nowhere, of course. But on the other hand, it is having an effect. Of cleansing the world, of clearing whole complexes away."

"We only share the world. We share it with time, which keeps growing. We have to change in time."

"He is a priest wandering in our ashes."

"Roi?"

No one moved in any way.

"Our destiny is to tell each other stories."

"Remember the day the dogs ran amuck?"

"My father was taking me to the Peacock Garden, we were standing on the platform waiting for the train. Down the track on which the express train runs, my dog came lumbering along. I tried to call out to it, but I couldn't. It seemed so enclosed within itself, exerting all its concentration to stay on the deadly crack. Stupid! I tried to scream. But my mouth would not operate. And then it flashed inside of me: he *is* stupid. And still I couldn't move. What was horrifying was his concentration. He was completely unaware of me. He passed out of sight and I remained there hardly moving, waiting for the inevitable, staring at the tracks and the embankment. After ten minutes the dog reappeared, lumbering in the opposite direction, enclosed by the same look as before. My father seemed not to have noticed anything at all. Was he holding it in like me? I was still unable to speak. Then our train pulled in and soon we were at the Peacock Garden. Full of the glory of colors, I made myself stop thinking about it, about the sight of my dog running on that track."

"To me that was the worst part. How you can walk into a garden and accept the garden instead of the world."

"All over the world it was happening."

"And I have never met anyone who saw anything except his own dog running on that track."

We looked at our bodies and imagined it was once and we were telling stories in the sand.

"Nothing comes together the same way anymore."

"We have chosen to be dead."

The confusions and crucifixions of the dream, slowly filling the spaces of the sand, slowly gathering ourselves in.

"In Europe the trains began arriving down those tracks."

"And we were delivered here."

"We have to keep remembering that."

We could feel that Roi was preparing himself to come over. He is dying to give us our injections. The moment he took his first step, we stood and moved into the game room. Our feet, in the slippers we have to wear, make our footsteps sound a little like the wind. We are still afraid, but less so now. We have learned how to keep our faces empty and are beginning to control our eyes and our breath.

"He thinks he's a Semite. Ask him what his name is."

"What the fuck does he know about being a Semite?"

"Nothing."

CLUMP 11

(Rambo's play)

HAMLET LOOSE

A heavy black woman, black dress, no shoes, sits, floor level,
on the floor, legs drawn up, arms around them, despondent,
despairing, unhelpable, unreachable. Stage (or floor) right
is dark.

Woman: Dream. Alone on ship. Looking at woman on
operating table. Suddenly realizes is expected to give birth.
I notice she isn't pregnant. Struggles. Suddenly realizes
they are putting the baby *into* her. Screams. Suddenly
realize. Suddenly realize. *My* body. Struggle. Corpse giving
birth. Not right! Not right! Every night. Alone on ship.
Afraid. Woman being operated on. They have *put* the baby
in. Dead. Giving birth to their baby. Dead. *My* body. My
body. Operating. *Give me my body.* Corpse giving birth.
My baby! (She is immobile, a weight, a pressure.)

Director: What follows is not fundamentally a script. What
is essential here is the notion of a company, not a cast. The
woman's words, as meaning, as sound, her physical being, her
pain, are a kind of organizing metaphor around which the
company comes together (or avoids coming together). The
script, as such, can be taken as a script or it can be used as
just a for instance. Anyone can change his lines. The actors
are free, unbound. The script I have provided sees them,
once they are free, as being free of the personal death of the
Hamlet script. They are alive within the circle of the myth, but
each has hitherto been neglected by the play, each has his own
individual outcry and his own individual destiny to attend
to. Each is as important to himself as Hamlet. The play
is a coming to consciousness—that is, the play *is* the

59

breaking loose *from* the play, the emergence into life,
freedom of every character. If you like, the full emergence
into a Hamlet play of *every* character in the life play.

Laertes and Ophelia, off by themselves, talking.

Ophelia: Do you doubt?
Laertes: For Hamlet and the trifling of his favor, hold it
a fashion and a toy in blood, a violet in the youth of primy
nature, forward, not permanent, sweet, not lasting, the
perfume and suppliance of a minute, no more.
Ophelia: No more, but so?
Laertes: Think it no more. For nature crescent does not
grow alone in thews and bulks, but as this temple waxes
the inward service of the mind and soul grows wide withal.
Perhaps he loves you now, and no soil nor cautel doth
besmirch the virtue of his will. Yet you must fear. (They
kiss. Exit Laertes.)
Ophelia: I shall the effect of this good lesson keep, but
do not as some ungracious pastors do, show me the steep
and thorny way to heaven, whiles like a puffed and reckless
libertine, himself the primrose path of dalliance treads and
recks not his own rede. (Exits.)

Hamlet and Gertrude. They are in the midst of talking.

Queen: O Hamlet, mine eyes turn into my very soul, and
there I see such black and grained spots as will not leave
their tinct.
Hamlet: Nay, live on in the rank sweat of an unseamed
bed, stewed in the corruption, honeying and making love
over the nasty sty.
Director: A wall. A great many hooks, the kind

60

that are used for putting bookshelves on, have been screwed
into it. A man hangs from one of the hooks. His wrists and
ankles have been bound loosely. He begins, slowly, moving
from hook to hook. There is enough span between the wrists
for him to utilize the rope length as a climbing tool. Progress
will necessarily be erratic. He will have to go down and up
as well as across. All he can do is catch on to the nearest
hook. He can rest whenever he wants by putting his feet on
one of the hooks. Whenever the strain of moving hook by
hook across the wall becomes too great, he can, if he is not
conserving his strength altogether, breathe loudly, grunt,
make whatever his *real* sound and effort are. Like the
woman, he is one of the play's interpretations, one of its
two expressive predicaments. (Spot. He slowly moves.)

Queen: O, speak to me no more. These words like daggers
enter in mine ears.   No more, sweet Hamlet.
Hamlet: A murderer and a villain, a slave that is not a
twentieth part ....
Black actor: (Who has been sort of casually eavesdropping.)

Hamlet: (Continuing without any interruption.) ...the
tithe of your precedent lord, a vice of kings, a cutpurse of the
empire and the rule, that from a shelf the precious diadem
stole and put it in his pocket....
Queen: No more.

Enter the Ghost in a ragged white robe.

Black Actor:

Hamlet: A king of shreds and patches—save me and hover
over me with your wings, you heavenly guards! What would
your gracious figure?

Queen: Alas, he's mad.

Hamlet: Do you not come your tardy son to chide, that, lapsed in time and passion, lets go by the important acting of your dread command?

Queen: Alas, how is it with you, that you do bend your eye on vacancy, and with the incorporeal air do hold discourse?

Exit Ghost, without speaking. Perhaps a minute without movement or sound. He re-enters.

Queen: On nothing. On nothing. (Distracted, anguished.) Whereon do you look Hamlet?

Enter ghost of Polonius. The two ghosts are dressed alike.

Ghost 2:   A rat. My daughter's father and he could say that I was a rat.

Black actor: (Re-enters. To Queen. Angrily.)

Queen: (Still in the text.) To whom do you speak, Hamlet? Tell me what I can do?

Director: Listen to *me*. Truth is obedience.

Queen: Someone *listen* to me. I want to have my baby.

Laertes: I want to have a prince's life.

Hamlet: Marry a princess, then.

Ophelia: The same dream all the time. *My* baby. My *body*.

Black actor 2:

Queen: Isn't there anyone here who understands? I *need* to have a baby.

Black actor 1:

Ghost 1:   Now I see the *whole* picture.

Queen: (To Black actor 1.) Why can't you have a baby with me?

62

Black actor 1:

Ghost 2:   (To Ghost 1.) You look to me like a father.
Queen: (To Black actor 1.) Yes. Like a father.
Horatio: (To Hamlet.) Is there anything I can do, my
prince?
Hamlet: Kill a father, marry a princess.
King: Can you understand? A life given over entirely to
the truth.
Rambo:

King: (Declaiming.) My play: The Natural Fear of the Dark.
Rambo:
Hamlet: Ah don' know, but I think I found a goose.
Black actor 1:
King: See? See? This is Central Pain. You are all in
Pain. Please laugh. Thank you. Do not applaud. Thank you.
There can be no performance without pre-established response.
Repeat. There can be no performance without pre-established
response.
Guildenstern: Next time we get rid of the directors.
Rambo:

Ophelia: The same dream. Giving birth to *their* dead
baby. Hamlet, did you ever love *me*?
Queen: *I* want a baby, Hamlet.
Ophelia: Hamlet, why couldn't you just have loved me?
Black actor 2:

King: Not correct. Art is obedience. There is no disobedience
pattern. Art cannot be life. Will you laugh please. Thank
you. Will you cry please. Thank you. There can be no

performance without pre-established response. Disobedience
converts to pain. Will you smile please. Thank you.
Applaud please. Thank you. There is no disobedience
pattern.

Black actor 2:

Ophelia: Ssh. Have pity.

Hamlet: Narcissus had a face. How can I find it? Is that
what you think? Is Hamlet Narcissus, looking for a face
that will recall him? Like those worn-out men in all-night
cafeterias, mistaking first one face and then another for
their own? They walk out stifling the feeling of horror that
the face they wear is a stranger's.

Guildenstern: Then art is *dis*obedience. Art is *life*.
Were you unaware that there are people who *cannot* stand
to live in mirrors?

Ophelia: Ssh. He knows. He's *lost* in the mirror.

Hamlet: We die the way Apaches die: willingly, quietly.

Guildenstern: Next time we get rid of *all* the directors.
They *all* stand for control.

Black actor 1:

Horatio: I know all about you. Christ was blue.

Black actor 1:

Horatio: Deep Jew.

Laertes: Bring me my Sister back, whoever she was.

Hamlet: The best art is silent, like a mask.
King: Contend, contend, thou powers of truth.
Rambo:

CLUMP 12

"I can see how inevitably our position led us into seeking refuge in these houses of the dead. We needed time. We needed to prepare. But the barges. The stories have never been clear about that. Why do the barges enter in?"

"As the result of an idea and the personal style of a single man. Whoever he was, as I see it, the change must have come over him first. Then somehow all of us, each one of us, must have realized what a signal that could be, what a language we had at our disposal, and the force that this language of ours could generate."

"You mean different from the language we are using at this moment?"

"Not now. Not language in this context. I'm speaking of force, the force it takes to come back. This is in-gathering, here, now, in this imitation death. Who knows what language is? Language is a neural impulse, transmitted genetically, that unravels over thousands of years. This unravelling, this language, is our entire history. The barges were this unravelling, and the singing in the trains. This time of the imitation death is also part of that unravelling."

"The latest curse is to have survived into a time when our last story has no more meaning."

"Unimportant."

"There are too many stories."

"None alike."

"Tell us the story of the barges, then, and after about the trains."

"You have to imagine this man. You have to imagine him fully."

"Unravelling."

"Yes, unravelling. Suffering and unravelling. Not that he was better than anyone else, not that his pain was better than anyone else's. Neither. Only that words had changed for him, he experienced his life as a different language. The word message

67

had ceased to be inert. The word return had ceased to be inert. The word cancel had ceased to be inert. The world had become a total language, every one of its words, every sentence used or heard, caught fire in his mind and burned there."

"You are the man you speak of."

"It doesn't matter. Forget about me and think about what happened. You mustn't imagine that he was a superior being. He was like anyone. Then events happened and he was *changed*. His *time* had changed. If he was me, he was no longer me. He belonged completely to his *time*."

"Did he die?".

"No, not then. Not at that time. You have to see him as he was. Separated from his wife for a year. Renting a room from her in the back of an apartment that she lived in with her boy friend. A clumsy five-foot-eight-inch giant, there in a house like that. He couldn't deal with himself. And then in the morning he would be changed again, now into a five-foot-eight-inch dwarf. By seven o'clock he had exchanged tortures. A changeling angel is what he was. He would fill his mail sack, too large and too heavy, and do his daily rounds. He delivered letters. But the words had begun to change in his head. The bag was too heavy. He could not deliver. He couldn't deal with it. He could not deliver anything.

"The pleas for help, the messages of forgiveness, the outcries of children, of parents, of lovers. The cries were unceasing and multiplied day by day. The sickness was beyond cure. He took the letters home and put them in cartons, carefully marking the date on the outside."

"The boxes of mail filled the room. He looked at them numbly. As facts. As harbingers. Sooner or later . . . but he did not really want to. Sooner or later he would rouse himself. Sooner or later he would find a place. Sooner or later he would get rid of the letters."

"Tomorrow. He would begin mailing the letters tomorrow.

Let them suspect whatever they pleased. He would drop them in the mailboxes, a few at a time. Whenever he went out he would remail the letters. There was *always* a tomorrow."

Hero: The cartons had accumulated into too many tomorrows. I left the post office. For three days I still continued to carry letters, boxes full instead of sacks. I took them, and placing them carefully in chronological sequence, put them on board a garbage barge.

"Floated the barge out to sea. And then came here."

"I think he must have set that boat adrift because there was someone he would never set sail without."

"I won't say that you're wrong. But it wasn't who you think it was."

"It was someone he hadn't died for yet."

Heroine: Close your eyes. Then open them, you'll see an exact psychological map.

Hero: And you won't be here anymore. I never close my eyes.

Heroine: Don't be afraid of the dream. This is my freedom too. Or I wouldn't be here now.

Story-teller: The messages are still floating there. Pain burns into time, becomes part of the universe. But the senses of the living are weak. Their memories burn out more quickly.

Heroine: My people say that death is a place where a spell is put on the living so they can no longer remember where their faces are. Then they are confined to a house there in the place of death, where they have to remain until their faces have been found.

"Is there any way of recovering their faces and leaving the place of death?"

"Only if the spell wears off and the person remembers by himself. But there are many people in the same house, and mirrors are placed all over in order to deceive the confined and lead them to select the wrong face. Whoever chooses a face that is not his own goes mad instantly and loses all knowledge

69

of himself. Then he is truly dead, and forfeits forever the hope of living again."

"Here we have hidden our faces ourselves, so that only we can say where they are. In order to erase the spell that has been put on us."

"In our *own* time we'll put them on again."

Jaguar: But beware of glass and whatever else reflects.

Skull: Especially you, when you reach the sea. When you see yourself reflected in the water, the way the sun has made your eyes burn, it can cause you to imagine that you have become a giant. The sea can cast many spells. Do not forget who you are. You are not as far-seeing as the sun.

Stone: In this way the arrogant go mad. In this way their downfall is assured. I could claim to be a god too, when the sun causes my strength to burn. But at night when the sun goes into his house, in spite of my strength I shiver helplessly.

Wood: Remember the house inside yourself. The sun can cause a wind to spring up that will go through all the doors of your house. When a man's bones rattle like sticks of wood, there is no sea reflected in his eyes. When the sun wishes to kill some creature, first he causes it to turn into wood.

Emptiness: Do not allow yourself to be frightened by the other things of the world. They have no understanding. This makes them envious, because they imagine that the sun will grant you special favors.

"Teloca, do your people ever speak about those who do return?"

"They think of it as another spell. They speak of the return as the second life and compare it to a dream. Fools are said to be dreamers."

Then we were all laughing together. Teloca too.

"So do we think of it that way, too. We always knew that we were fools."

"What about our music? Are we taking our music?"

70

"What about our bodies? Are we taking our bodies?"

"Our music began in the ice, in the frost, we are traveling toward the sun."

"Our music began in the trains, in the cold, it came from bodies dying of the cold. The sun may be able to soften it. The return has taken a long time. Our history began in the sun, has maybe always been moving back to it. Look: every one of us possesses a song. Who has ever heard himself sing? Who has heard anyone else's singing? The unravelling of that sound throughout our time may be the only justice in all our deaths. I myself would be willing to settle for that."

"I remember the beggars on the subways. I used to want to collect money, bills. Lots of them. Or sometimes I would think maybe a dollar here, a dollar there. Five dollars occasionally. Once in a while a ten. Then I wanted to write on them: Get out of town, White Eye. And put the star underneath. Then you just feed them in. At theaters. On the subway. In restaurants. How long before it took effect? How long before it changed how we thought about art? How long before so many accumulated, there was nothing else in circulation? I even thought I had invented the words . . . whitey . . . White Eye . . . I couldn't get those faces out of my mind."

Story-teller: We have passed through deserts, we have walked on glaciers, and now we are almost alive again. There are nine deaths we have died, nine deserts in which we have perished, and then a final life. In the ninth desert, it was the desert of all talk. The words were like grains of rice, the sound of the voices was like teeth chewing against them, pulverizing the rice. It was the last desert to be gotten through. People talked incessantly, the noises grated and squeezed against each other. This was the worst of our ordeals. Each time someone spoke, the person listening would think of killing him. People spoke without letup and the only thought was of killing.

"I never gave singing a second thought. I was starving. Then

I was walking through the train singing. It was the most natural thing in the world. Then somehow it changed: I *saw* that money falling on the floor. People weren't *giving*, they were throwing it, letting go of it. I felt strange after that, self-conscious. I thought: what kind of ego could a person have to just stand up and sing like that? Some loud, happy, dumb song. What a grotesque irony. What a double grotesque irony. I was on my hands and knees on the floor thinking that. I don't know, maybe you do understand, wanting to write on all that money like that. The music I sang! Is that what blues are? Or was that blues *after?* My people invented blues. I ought to know the answer. But I don't. I had always sung before. Not for money. But wherever I was, on trains, anyplace. I don't think I could sing like that again. Not even for my life."

"We were starving also, but we don't have the same hungers. We don't mean the same thing by music. The music is always a voice, always connected with someone's voice. With us the singing has always been underground, on trains or in the subways. The throat constricts, but the lips never part, the mouth never opens. We hear it, but differently. The song stays inside the throat. You can hear it *in the trains* is the difference. You watch the throat constrict, and from all the cars you can feel it pouring as the trains flash on past."

The above was the final myth that we made, then and there, out of the talking, to capsulize it.

CLUMP 13

(It is the presence of death that prevents us from· calling this a living theater. Why should we continue to elevate degradation? What are we doing if not struggling to overcome the theater? Why should we wait? Why should we continue to use words that have no power to summon things? We have stories of our own to tell. Art is the struggle to overcome something, it is muscular action, there has to be something toppled. Art opposes monuments. We crave movement, air, a death in real light: as whales die, facing the sun, the mouth open.)

Polis 3. Following the Inquest Concerning the Disturbances at
the Card House.   I was no longer Teacher.   Her necessity
was strong. I was weak.   I had to leave
the Card House. I had to begin again.   It was required.

No one could have known that pictures of Blanche Neige
would be on four of the cards. **The four queens had the face
of Blanche Neige.**   Her necessity was stronger than mine.
    I had to leave the Card House. My luck was bad.

I was the most ignorant man in the village. In the whole vastness
I did not know when to kneel before the figures.   I did not
know their names. I did not know when one avoided them.
    I did not know how to ask. I did not know about any thing.

**In the future we will relate to the energy source more directly,
in ways beyond the spiritual.**

I watched the people and I was unable. There was no way
        that the village could tell. My ignorance was vaster than
            the land. We have to continue learning
                                                speaking
                With the force of wild cards.

CLUMP 14

I ran through the tunnels shouting her name, looking for her. Echoes converged, muffled me. I kept trying to get out. I still remembered her. We were two different words. Teloca. Myself. I am outside the tunnel. There is no Teloca.

CLUMP 15

BLUE WOMB

The dining room of a Grand Hotel. Solid bourgeois plush.
Entertainment. While being entertained, the guests are eating
desserts, drinking coffee, relaxing. Juju has curly red
hair, is of medium height and stocky build, muscular and
tending slightly toward flab. He is nude except for a jockstrap
and a well-stuffed knapsack on his back. He struts rather than
walks, and his manner is altogether arrogant. The dining
room goès from left to right across the stage. Juju is at
the front, stage left. All the way to the rear, stage right, on a
slightly raised dais, is Odessa. His hair is dark, he wears a
perfectly trimmed goatee, a black and white checked jacket,
and is sipping from a glass of red wine. He constantly takes
his napkin, which is white linen, and pats his lips with it.
Before patting his lips, however, he is fairly conspicuous about
rolling it into a ball first. A second guest worth noting is a
thin, aristocratic but at the same time very dissipated-looking
man. He is very nervous, constantly pushing his hair back and
moistening his lips with his tongue. Last, a woman, extremely
overdressed, middle to late thirties, wearing a red dress with
which she has combined a chain necklace with a Byzantine
cross strikingly outlined with pearls.

Juju: I may say, without delivering a polemic upon the
subject, that in the last decade our attitude toward the body has
undergone a fundamental change. There are things we take for
granted now which once, astonishing though it may seem, all
our instincts would have tempted us to deny. For example, these
childish bodies of ours, the sight of which we once considered
so provocative that one is forced to conclude they must have
been regarded as a challenge to something deep within us. Or
to some deeply venerated belief we held, perhaps without even

79

the knowledge that we held it. And as for deformity, that too we have learned to take a more intelligent attitude toward. The Hindus tell us there is no such thing as good or evil. Though our poor culture has perhaps not advanced that far in understanding, we have at least come far enough to make a beginning, to begin to think about ourselves clinically, unemotionally. Eh? Is it possible that beauty and ugliness, like good and evil, like will and no will, are also illusions. (Laughs.) Yes, we are living in an age when the body is no longer the soul's prison. (Pauses.) Is it possible that ugliness no longer exists? Eh? That we have succeeded in banishing it from the world? (To Odessa.) I ask the devotee of the vine, the gentleman in the rear. Is it possible that my body is pleasant to see? Eh? (He approaches Odessa, hands on hips, mincing, strutting, putting on, parading every aspect of his physicality.) Can you speak? Speech is the first of the gifts of civilization. It is the constant delight of man. And of woman. Let us never forget woman. All that has come into being, the best of all we possess, rises in testimony that the skills of the tongue are the greatest of man's delights. And woman's. Eh? (Bows in the direction of the lady in red.) Speech is the fairest of the arts. Look. Look at me. Here I hold you rapt, enthralled, and all through the power of my tongue. Eh? Admit it. Eh? (Back and forth in front of Odessa's table. Laughs.) Well? What do you say regarding my question? Have you a tongue in *your* head?

Odessa: Why are they disinfecting the city?

Juju: Routine, of course. Mere routine. Orders from the police. Orders from above. For no reason. For show only. Why does disinfectant upset you?

Odessa: I will not be insulted by the likes of you.

Juju: Eh? Well. Do you prefer the plague? Did you come to die in our city? You could be accommodated. There is a

80

certain street I know. Are we such strangers to your ways that you cannot see when a benevolent authority is only interested in protecting you?

Odessa: From what? Who is dying in the city?

Juju: Why we all are. Eh? (Turns and walks to the front of the room, ie stage left again. He begins to chant.)

> In the city
> Out in the streets
> The city is dying
> Out in the streets
>
> The people are changing
> Out in the streets
> The city is changing
> The people are dying
> Out of the city
> Out of the streets

(He walks over to the aristocratic-looking man's table.) Now *there* is a man with a tongue in his head. I need your mouth in my service. Put your tongue in *my* head. Eh? In my hand then. (Laughs.) Come. Sing to my tune. My mouth will shape your expression. (They repeat the chant in unison, Juju forcing him.) Eh? Eh? (Laughs again.) Open your mouth. Keep it open. Now! Sing!

Aristocrat: (With Juju.)

> The city is dying
> Out in the streets
> The people are changing
> Out in the streets

81

The people are dying
Out in the streets

(The Aristocrat attempts to stop.)
   Juju: Not yet! Continue!

Dying
Down in the city
Dying
Down in the people

(The Aristocrat once more attempts to stop.)
   Juju: Again!

Down in the city
Dying
Down in the people
Dying

(While the Aristocrat is attempting to go on, Juju changes
his own lines.)

Everything will change
in a moment
The second tree will appear
in a moment
It will be
the second life
It will dawn
for those who believe
It will be the last
Words of God.

(Hands on hips, strutting arrogantly.) Well? Applaud the
gentleman. Is this what he gets for his labor? Is this what
music is worth to you?

Dignified Man: What sort of music is this?

Juju: *My* sort of music. *And* his. (Points to the Aristocrat.)
Kindly remember that *he* is a gentleman, and that though
you are entirely lacking in *common* courtesy—eh?—you are
bound to respect *him*. Eh? (Waits.) So this is what our society
is coming to? No *exalted* courtesy either?
Where is your applause for a gentleman who has
entertained you? I ask again. Is that what the art of
entertainment is worth to you? A closed mouth?
(Applause. To the Aristocrat.) See? They liked your song.
You are a borne entertainer. Eh? Now show your appreciation
of them. Come. Stick out your tongue at them. Well, come.
Fair is fair. They applauded you. Now salute them. (Firmly.)
Stick-out-your-tongue-at-them.

Guest: What is this?

Juju: Why what do you think? An exhibition. (To the
Aristocrat.) Come, my exhibitionist. Eh? (Laughs.) Eh?
Stick-out-your-tongue.

Aristocrat: (Sticks out his tongue.)

Juju: A man of parts, of many hats, and a true
gentleman. Even your tongue is coated. You may put it
back where it came from. (Laughs.)

Guest 2: This is insufferable.

Juju: Insufferable! You exaggerate, I assure you, I guarantee,
you can bear it. Come ladies and gentlemen, fair is fair once
again. After all, consider how much I have had to bare on
your behalf. Eh? (Struts, hands on hips.) Well? Now is your
chance to have your say. Come. The entertainment is finished.
For this evening, I bid you good night. Now, to show me
the manliness, and the womanliness, eh?, of your opinions,

83

to show me that your complaints are to be taken seriously,
all of you stick your tongues out at me. (Walks from side
to side in front of them.) Come now. Eh? Stick your tongues
out at me. (Staring at her necklace, walks toward the woman
in red.) Well madam? Eh? I am not afraid to stick my
tongue out at you. (Does so.) I am your humble and very
own pearl diver. Well? You will not reciprocate? Kiss my
hump, at least. For luck. No? Ah! I am not so ungentle-
manly as you are unwomanly. My tongue is entirely at
the service of your own mound. (Sticks his tongue out.)
Those tongues will be wagging soon enough. Why
so sluggish now?

Odessa: They are disinfecting the city. Why?

Juju: I ask you, ladies and gentlemen, why is this
stranger in our midst so preoccupied with disinfectant?
Instead of attacking our fair city, can you explain yourself
and the suspicions in your own mind? Can you explain your
suspicious mind?

Odessa: Explanations to the clown? You've merely
been hired to amuse us.

Juju: But you are not so simply amused, you
complicated man. Moreover, you misunderstand the nature
of this performance. Is it not rather you who are providing
the *amusement*? No answer? A big mouth. Much cheek but
little behind it. Much cheek but little tongue in it. Eh? Then
to show you that *I* know how to appreciate entertainment,
I will salute *you* for *your* show. (Sticks his tongue out,
waggles it around and around.)

Odessa: I haven't given you any show. Red devil.

Juju: Haven't you? Soon you will have a craving to give all
that you now so proudly hold on to. How do you like that for
a fortune-telling show?

Odessa: *I* will not make *your* fortune if you tell and show
in that fashion.

Juju: Eh? Bravo! See? Already you begin to feel stirrings

inside. Eh? Did truth not come from my mouth?

Odessa: You wouldn't speak to me in that fashion if you were standing where I could reach you. Red devil.

Juju: So you imagine me standing already? Are you ready to go for me so soon? Caro! If you make a prophet *of* me, you will make a profit *for* me. I *will* make my fortune if I tell and show in this wise. Eh? And then you are profitless and no prophet at all. Eh, my proud and complex gentleman?

Odessa: I don't know. And I will no longer dignify your incredible rudeness by engaging you any further in talk.

Juju: You have broken our engagement? Caro! How my heart longs for you. Eh? And what is there within the circle of your self that longs as much for me? Nothing? Nothing that longs at all? (Laughs.) This outward show of hardness bespeaks that you are too easily touched, eh? (Laughs uproariously.) As innocent as a lens!

A distracted-looking man, naked to the waist, enters the dining room. He walks through, apparently looking for someone. He turns in a circle once or twice, looking all the while. When he gets about ten feet from Odessa's table, and facing to the left of it, he gets down on his knees. Looking completely absorbed, he remains on his knees for about thirty seconds. He gets up, still looking distracted, and leaves from where he entered.

Guest 1: This is shameless.

Guest 2: The management must be held responsible.

Guest 3: My God, how everything has declined here. When you think of what this hotel used to be. My God!

Juju: Declined? Yes. It is now in the genetive.

Guest 1: If the city is being disinfected, what are you doing here?

Juju: Manners, ladies and gentlemen. Respect. A small

85

beginning. Hold only your tongues. Eh? Consider our
Mediterranean heritage, and that our forebears always
venerated what was behind them. And so they grew great.
A small beginning often goes a long way.

   Odessa: Answer his question! What are you doing here?

   Juju: Why struggling for control of your tongue. And now
answer my question. If.the city is disinfecting outside, who is
disinfecting the inside? So. For the present, then, I leave
all that is behind you, all that is before you, and all that
is between you in this gentleman's hands. (Indicates Odessa.
Cups his hands beneath his tongue and wags it. Laughs.)

   Woman:

Whoever is "it" needs to be cool. Needs to have a
strategy. Has to work and play well with others. Be satisfactory
in conduct. Has to have a good attitude. Clean body and a
healthy mind. Or else the others will run too fast. Or else the
others will stay in their hiding places. If they don't come out,
you have to stay "it". If you can't catch up with them, you have
to stay "it". If they tag you right back, you have to stay "it".
And come again another day.